Imagine!
Imagine! © 2013 by Diane Winn
Illustrations © 2013 by Patty Reddy
All rights reserved.

Printed in the United States of America

For information write
Diane Winn
www.througheagleseyes.com

Printed in the United States

ISBN# 0-000000-0-0

For Kate, Lily, Mae, Landon and Brooks,

In Joy,

Diane Winn

Once upon a time there was a little girl named Lucy. Lucy was kind and funny, smart and playful.

She was also strong-willed, stubborn and liked to have her way. She was not unlike most anyone else. Lucy was unique and special...

just like you.

One morning as Lucy was getting ready for her day, she looked out her bedroom window and saw her good friend Hannah playing with Juan. Lucy was disappointed that she had not been invited to play.

She went downstairs to find her mom. "It's not fair, Mommy! Hannah is playing with Juan! They didn't invite me!" Lucy said as she hung her head and tears began to form.

Her very wise mother said, "Perhaps this is a day that you would like to find something else to do. Take a slow deep breath with me. Let it out just as slowly. Now, use your imagination. What other things can you do that are fun?"

"I know!" exclaimed Lucy. "I'll call Charlie and see if he can play."

The very next day, Lucy and Ollie were working on an art project at the recreation center. Ollie didn't want to share his box of crayons. Lucy went to find the teacher. "It's not fair!" exclaimed Lucy. "Ollie won't share his crayons!"

Her very wise teacher said, "Perhaps you could use your very creative imagination to find a solution."

After a slow deep breath, in and out, Lucy exclaimed "I know! I'll use the markers at the art table!"

A few days later, Lucy and her grandfather began to prepare dinner. "Let's make guacamole" Lucy suggested. "That is a very good idea" said her grandfather, "except we have no avocados." "It's not fair!" exclaimed Lucy. "I wanted guacamole with our dinner!"

Her very wise grandfather said "Why don't we take a slow deep breath together. In and out. Then, use your very creative imagination and figure this out."

Lucy and her grandfather took a breath. Lucy paused for a moment, then she turned to her grandfather and said, "I know! We can have hummus with our dinner instead!"

On Saturday, Lucy woke up. She was looking forward to a day of play. When she came to the kitchen for breakfast, her father said, "There are a few chores that need to be done before you go out to play. The first is to clean your room."

Lucy was very sad. She did not like to clean her room. She thought it was boring and hard work. She stuck out her bottom lip and put on a sad face.

After a moment, Lucy took a slow deep breath. In and out. All of a sudden a very wise Lucy smiled, looked up and said, "Dad, I think I'll use my creative imagination to find a way to make cleaning my room fun."